School Rules for Diva Duck

magic Wagon

BY **Janice Levy**

ILLUSTRATED BY
Colleen Madden

visit us at www.abdopublishing.com

Published by Magic Wagon, a division of the ABDO Group, PO Box 398166,
Minneapolis, MN 55439. Copyright © 2013 by Abdo Consulting Group, Inc.
International copyrights reserved in all countries. All rights reserved. No part of this
book may be reproduced in any form without written permission from the publisher.

Looking Glass Library™ is a trademark and logo of Magic Wagon.

Printed in the United States of America, North Mankato, Minnesota.
052012
092012
 This book contains at least 10% recycled materials.

Written by Janice Levy
Illustrations by Colleen Madden
Edited by Stephanie Hedlund and Rochelle Baltzer
Cover and interior design by Jaime Lint

Library of Congress Cataloging-in-Publication Data

Levy, Janice.
  School rules for Diva Duck / by Janice Levy ; illustrated by Colleen Madden.
    p. cm. – (Diva Duck)
  Summary: Diva Duck thinks that because she is talented, she does not have to
study or obey school rules.
  ISBN 978-1-61641-889-2
  1. Ducks–Juvenile fiction. 2. Animals–Juvenile fiction. 3. Schools–Juvenile fiction.
4. Fame–Juvenile fiction. (1. Ducks–Fiction. 2. Animals–Fiction. 3. Schools–Fiction. 4.
Fame–Fiction.) I. Madden, Colleen M., ill. II. Title.
  PZ7.L5832Sch 2012
  (E)–dc23
                              2011052031

The school bell rang.
Diva groaned as she ducked into class.

Hello, Class!
Today is

"School's for fools," she muttered.
"I am Diva Duck, destined for greatness!"

Diva showed off her new clothes.
She handed out copies of her latest CD.

She posed for pictures with her classmates.

She tweeted her fans:
Reading and writing — *not exciting*.

Everyone **quacked** up at her jokes, except Mr. Webb. The teacher called Diva to the board.

"What's ten plus ten?" he asked.

"**Ten too many**," Diva giggled.

Math? She tweeted. Don't count on it!

At lunchtime, Diva **pushed** ahead in line.
She danced across the tables.
She painted her name with ketchup.

"Where are your manners?"
Mr. Webb said. "Read the rules."

CAFETERIA RULES
* NO FOOD FIGHTS
* NO CUTTING IN LUNCH LINE
* NO PLAYING WITH YOUR FOOD
* NO BAD-MOUTHING VEGGIES, PLEASE
* CLEAN UP AFTER YOU EAT
← RECYCLE!

Diva looked at the chart but couldn't sound out the words.

Books are for schnooks, she tweeted.

When the school bell rang, Mr. Webb called to Diva, "Better study for tomorrow's spelling test."

"Word," said Diva, wiggling her butt.

"No hurries, no worries.
I am Diva Duck, **destined** for **greatness!**"

When Diva got home, she tossed her books away. She did high kicks.

She **sang** in the shower.

She **yakked** to her agent.

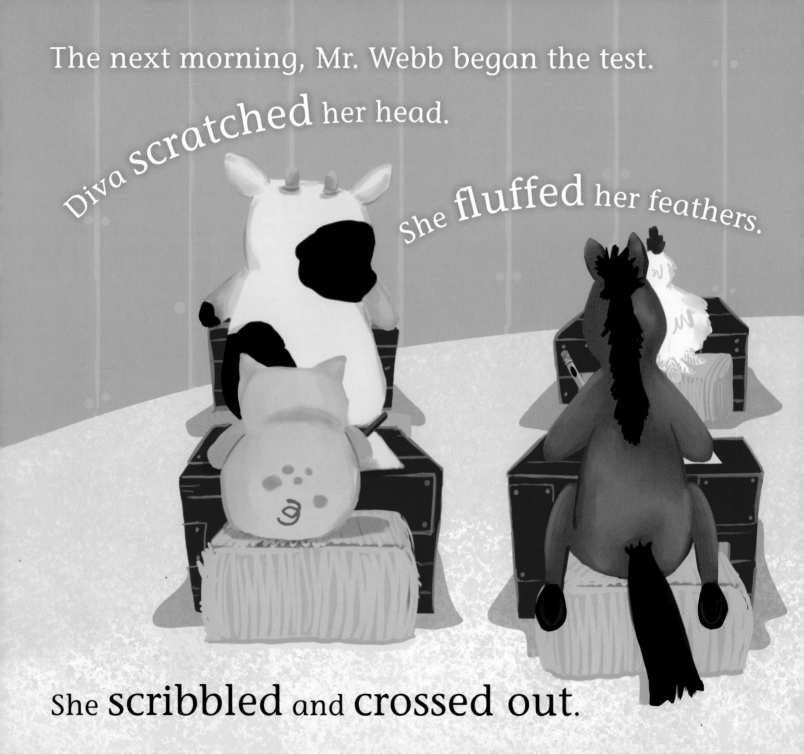

The next morning, Mr. Webb began the test.

Diva scratched her head.

She fluffed her feathers.

She scribbled and crossed out.

"No fun, I'm done," she gulped.

She didn't get anything right.
Word spread throughout the school.

"Diva can't write!" clucked the hens.

"Diva **can't** read!" snorted the pigs.

"She **still** counts on her toes!" the horses whinnied. **"Featherbrain!"**

Diva's wings drooped.
She belly flopped. She sank
to the bottom of the pond.

Her fans tweeted:

What's up with the duck?

That night Diva had a strange dream.
A tornado spun her tour bus through
the sky. It landed far away, in the
middle of a forest.

"Help, I'm lost!" Diva cried. "I can't read the map! How do I get to Hollywood?"

A wise owl answered, "Practice, practice, practice."

Diva jumped out of bed. She **splashed** water from the pond.

"I am Diva Duck!" she shouted. "I am destined for greatness!

I can dance.
I can sing.
I can do anything!"

Being smart takes heart, Diva tweeted her fans. **I won't let you down.**

From then on,
Diva studied her
math tables.

She learned her spelling words.

She read each night before going to bed.

"Did you study?" Mr. Webb asked before the next test.

"Piece of fish," Diva said, snapping her feathers. "I've got it covered."

This time she got everything right.
Diva high-fived her classmates.
Her hips went **boom-ducka-boom**.

The
BARNYarD
Players
Proudly
Present ...

Don't be slackers, my Little Quackers, Diva tweeted.

School Rules!

Diva Duck

★ At first, Diva Duck thought school was a waste of time. What changed her mind?

★ What are some of the things Diva couldn't do if she couldn't read, write, spell, or do math?

★ Diva was proud of herself when she passed the spelling test. Name one thing you worked hard for at school and were proud you accomplished.

About the Author: Janice Levy is the author of numerous award-winning children's books. Topics include bullying, multiculturalism, foster care, intergenerational relationships, and family values. She teaches creative writing at Hofstra University. Her adult fiction is widely published in magazines and anthologies.

About the Illustrator: Colleen Madden is an illustrator, mom, kickboxer, ukulele strummer, and honorary frog. She loves to draw for kids (and kids at heart!) and make people giggle. Diva Duck is her fourth series of children's books. She is currently writing her own titles as author/illustrator, which will all be very silly books.